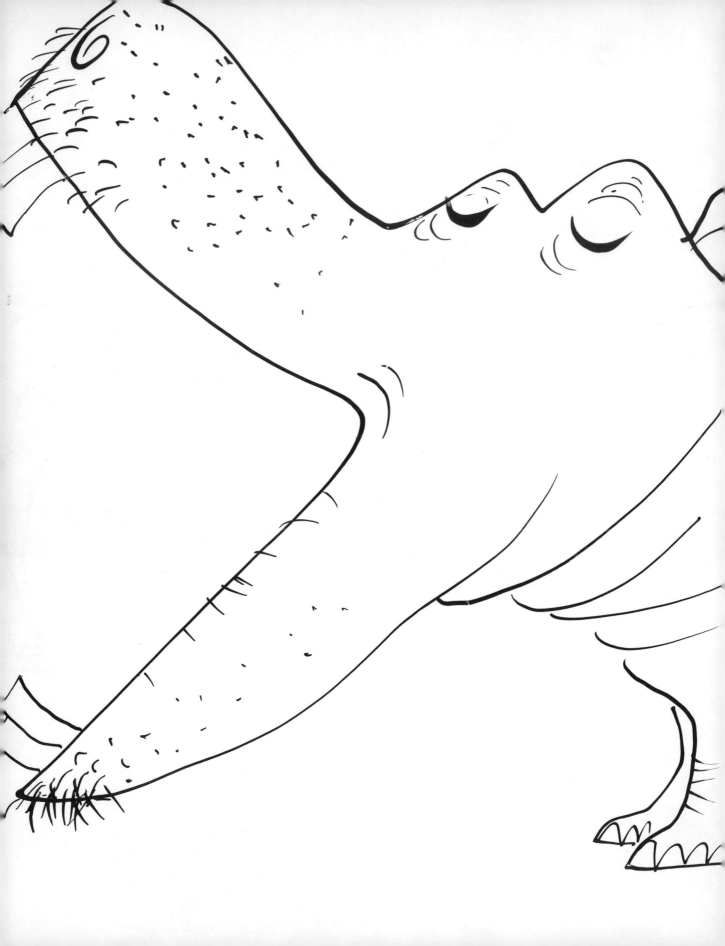

Veronica

Written and Illustrated by

ROGER DUVOISIN

ALFRED A. KNOPF  NEW YORK

This title was originally catalogued by the Library of Congress as follows:

Duvoisin, Roger
    Veronica; written and illus. by Roger Duvoisin. Knopf 1961
unp illus

    "Pity poor Veronica, the inconspicuous hippopotamus who
lives with so many hippopotamuses that she isn't noticed. Off
she goes to the city where she is unique, but also in the way,
until a nice lady comes along."   — Library Journal

    1. Hippopotamus — Stories   2. Picture books for children
I. Title

B 11-487   E
LJ Cards Inc © 1965   —p

Trade Ed.: ISBN: 0-394-81792-3   Lib. Ed.: ISBN: 0-394-91792-8

THIS IS A BORZOI BOOK, PUBLISHED BY ALFRED A. KNOPF, INC.

Veronica

Hippopotamuses can sometimes be very conspicuous.

But not so Veronica.
She was a most inconspicuous hippopotamus because
she lived with so many
mother and father hippopotamuses,
uncle and aunt hippopotamuses,
brother and sister hippopotamuses,
cousin hippopotamuses,
so many, that no one even knew Veronica was there.

"No one notices me here," she sighed unhappily. "I don't even know myself."

Not even the cool, muddy river bank, soft as a bed of feathers where she slept in the hot sun; the clear water in the middle of the river where she swam and splashed, could make Veronica happy.

"Oh," she sighed, "I want to be different . . . in fact, I would like very much to be *famous*."

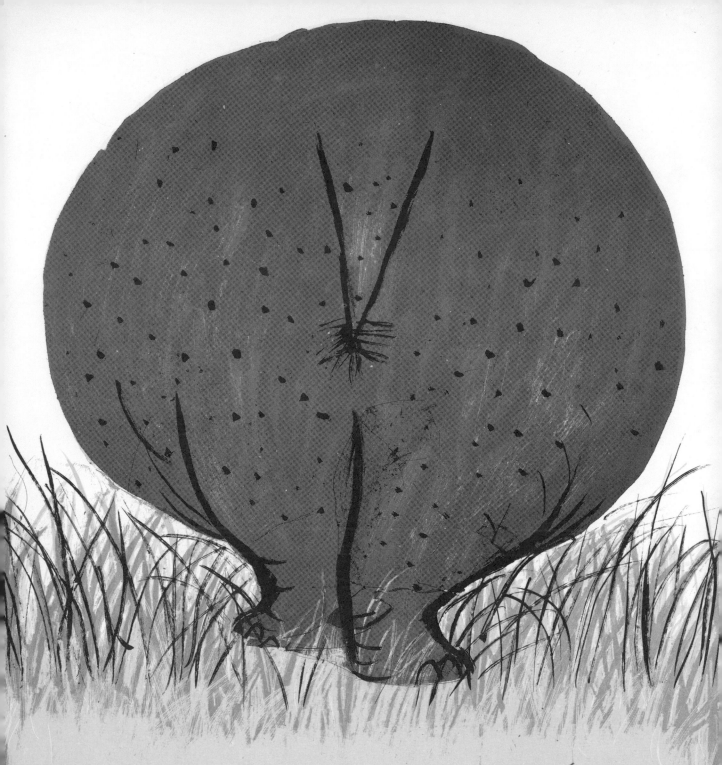

So Veronica walked away by herself, one day, to find a country
where she could be different . . . or even famous. She walked for days,
many many days, eating grass and leaves along the way.

One afternoon from the top of a hill she saw a pink and white city. The streets were crowded with men and women—even more crowded than Veronica's hippopotamus river.

When Veronica reached the streets of the city, she *knew* she was different. THERE WAS NOT ANOTHER HIPPOPOTAMUS IN SIGHT.

Only people, and more people, and still more people—people who stared at her, bumped into her, and shouted angrily at her when she stepped on their toes.

She was gloriously conspicuous.

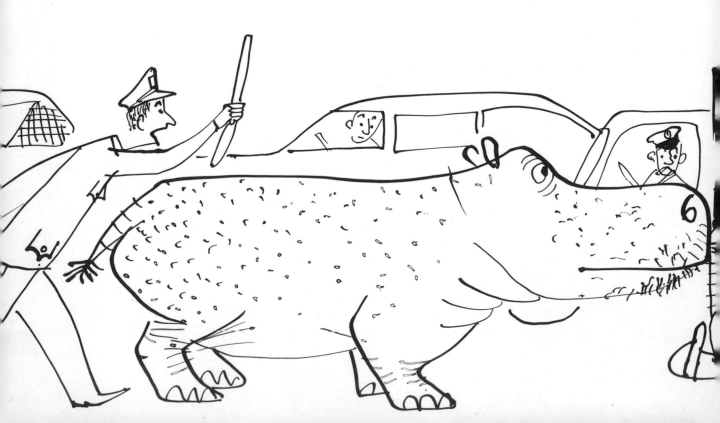

Veronica tried to walk in the middle of the street where there were no people. *But*—automobiles bumped into her, and horns blew angrily. Even the policeman blew his whistle, and scolded her.

"Lady," he said to Veronica, "this is a one way street, and you are going the wrong way."

Veronica turned around and followed the traffic. She felt very tired and sleepy and looked around for a place to rest.

There was no comfortable, soft mud bank, but Veronica thought the sidewalk looked cool. She stretched out and went to sleep, to dream happily of being a conspicuous hippopotamus . . . perhaps even a famous hippopotamus.

Now, Veronica was not only conspicuous; she was very much in the way, and was told to move on.

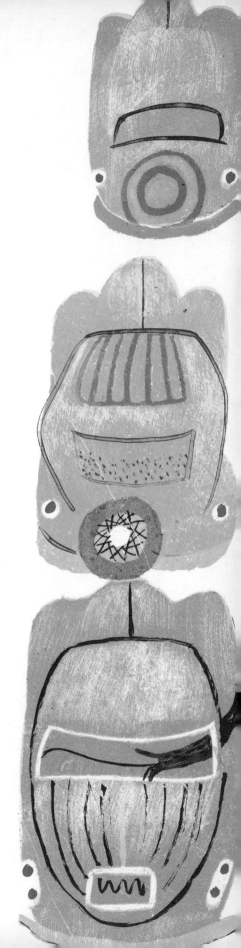

She obliged politely but with a sigh, for she was very tired. She went to lie down at the curb. It would do just as well as the sidewalk.

The Policeman, though, did not think so.

"Lady," he said once more, "don't you know that you cannot park in front of the fire hydrant?"

This time he took out his pad to give Veronica a ticket. But, being a nice man, he directed her to a place across the street where she could sleep quietly.

"I don't know how these people can sleep without mud or straw" said Veronica looking over the new place. "Still, it is very quiet here. And with these things on both sides of me it will be as if I slept between my brothers and sisters."

Even in her sleep Veronica was now so conspicuous that people gathered to look at her.

Now, even a conspicuous hippopotamus must have food, and water to drink and to splash in, and mud to wallow in.

The next morning, Veronica started out to look for these things. But she found nothing but streets and more streets and people who stared at her, bumped into her, and shouted angrily when she stepped on their toes.

Presently, she saw a shallow fountain in the middle of a square with just little red fish swimming round and round its edges.

"No people in the water?" wondered Veronica. "It must be that people do not drink water or take baths."

But Veronica waded into the fountain happily. She drank, she splashed noisily, and rolled on her back in the lovely cool water.

Out flew the fishes onto the sidewalk. Out splashed the water all over the people on the sidewalk. Soon the fountain was empty.

Veronica did not notice that people were angry with her now. She smiled with joy at the sight of a vegetable vendor who was walking by, pushing a cart full of fresh delicious cabbages, salads, beans, peas, potatoes, and many other things.

Unused to city manners, like all river bank hippopotamuses, Veronica helped herself happily to the green food. In one gulp, she emptied the cart clean.

"Thief! Thief!" screamed the vegetable vendor.

"Thief, thief, thief," echoed the crowd. "Arrest her!"

"What happened here?" shouted a policeman, hearing all the noise.

"She stole my cartful of vegetables," cried the vendor. "Cleaned it with one gulp. And all the paper bags too."

"Heavens," said the policeman, "one gulp?"

"One gulp! Look at her big mouth."

"Well then," said the policeman to Veronica, "you are under arrest. You step on people's feet; you stop the traffic; you bathe in a

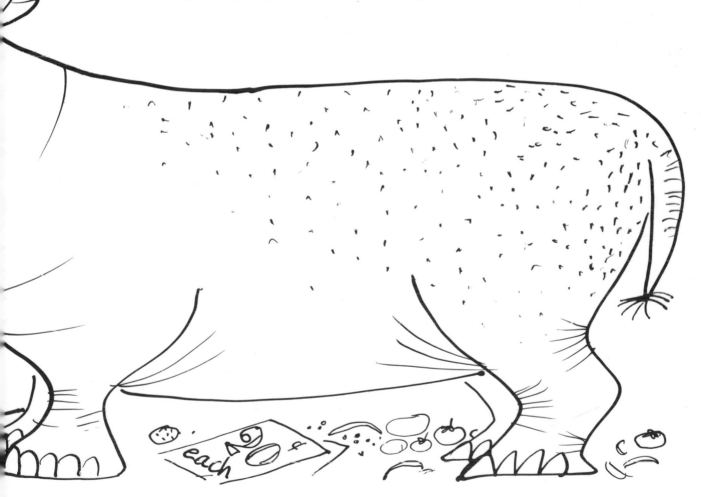

public fountain and dry up the city's fish; and now you steal . . . come along to jail."

Veronica did not know what a jail was, but the policeman's loud voice so frightened her that she pushed the crowd aside and galloped down the street with hippopotamus speed.

The policeman, the vendor, and everybody else ran after her. It seemed to Veronica as if the whole city was running at her heels.

"I must hide quickly or I am lost," she said, breathlessly. "These people surely want to beat me up."

At the end of the long street she saw a green park with trees, benches, and statues.

"I am saved," she thought. "I'll hide behind a bench and escape from this city when it's dark."

But even behind a bench, Veronica was still conspicuous.

She soon found herself with a rope around her neck and on her way to jail.

If Veronica had never seen a jail, the jail had never seen a hippopotamus. It had **NOT** been made for hippopotamuses. The door was too narrow for Veronica.

She could not go through it even with dozens of men pushing

from behind, and pulling from in front.

Finally, a bull-dozer was brought to help push Veronica through the door. With one push she was *in* the jail.

At that moment, a nice old lady came in too, and SHE scolded the policeman and the onlookers.

"Aren't you ashamed to do this to a poor hippopotamus! You should be locked up in jail yourselves."

"Madame," said the policeman, "she is a thief. She stole a whole cartful of vegetables."

"*My* vegetables," said the vendor.

The lady opened her bag and gave the vendor a bank note.

"Does this repay you for your vegetables?"

"Oh yes, Madame. Every one of them. Thank you."

"Very well then," said the nice old lady. "Officer, let this sweet hippopotamus out at once."

"I can't," said the policeman. "The door is too narrow and the bull-dozer cannot come in to push her out from behind."

"Then demolish the door," ordered the nice old lady. The door WAS demolished. Veronica was free!

The nice old lady also seemed to know very well that Veronica had
had enough of the city, and that she was tired of being conspicuous.
One can be *too* conspicuous.

"I only want to go home to my mud bank,' said Veronica, "to my

river, to all my hippopotamuses."

The lady ordered a moving van brought to move Veronica back to her country. And that was done too.

Veronica left the city as the policeman, the vendor, the little old lady, and all the people cheered her.

So, that was how Veronica wallowed again in the cool mud by the river bank, swam and splashed in the clear current, and slept among all the father, mother, brother, sister, aunt, uncle, cousin hippopotamuses.

But there was a difference.

She was now famous among hippopotamuses and beloved by all of them. Almost everyday at sunset they gathered around her to hear about her marvelous adventures in the pink and white city.

And Veronica was very happy.